THE PROPOSAL ACCEPTED

LOVING THE LIFE

BY

MOUMITA SAHA

 pencil

ISBN 978-93-5438-931-3

Published in India 2020 by Pencil

A brand of

One Point Six Technologies Pvt. Ltd.

123, Building J2, Shram Seva Premises,

Wadala Truck Terminal, Wadala (E)

Mumbai 400037, Maharashtra, INDIA

E connect@thepencilapp.com

W www.thepencilapp.com

Author biography

Myself, Moumita Saha, from Kolkata West Bengal, India.

Teacher | Story teller

As Charles W. Eliot righteously says "Books are the quietest and most constant of friends; they are the most accessible and wisest of counselors, and the most patient of teachers, "my present book is a compilation of five short stories that depict the values of relationship, love and mutual understanding in our daily lives and close relations and the lessons we learn from life. Ups and downs are inevitable, but we should have the resilience to face those challenges. Love plays an important role in building up our relations and togetherness makes it possible to meet all the challenges in life. The three C s – Courage, Confidence and Care are the basis of Love and Life.

Contents

ACKNOWLEDGEMENTS

This book is dedicated to my caring parents Mr. Chittaranjan Saha and Mrs Bela Saha and my loving husband Dr. Susanta Saha.

INTRODUCTION

"We were the people who were not in the papers. We lived in the blank white spaces at the edges of print. It gave us mopre freedom. We lived in the gaps between the stories."

Margaret Atwood, The Handmaid's Tale.

RELIEVED...

BANG!!!!!!!!

Ramu enters thrashing the door. Dadiji is watching television sitting on the sofa. Startled by the sound she asks "What happen Ramu? Why are you so exited?" Ramu is arranging the dinning table. He replies, "What to say Dadiamma! There is a tussle at the centre of the road. Some people have caught a 16-17 year old boy red handed, pickpocketing. They have tied him up and now awaiting the police to come". Dadiji mutes the sound of the television and goes towards the balcony. Anxiously asks Ramu, "Don't you think it's too late. Nitin should come back now!" Raju eyes at the clock. It's half past seven already. It's really late. Deadly he comments,"Dadiamma, it's so late. Nitin baba comes usually at six in the evening." Dadiji nods her head and leans slightly over the balcony. Again she asks Ramu, "Please go outside once again and look for him Ramu". Ramu sighs, "But Dadiamma you see I have just come from the grocery. Nitin Baba's no trace was there." Dadiji comes back on the sofa. She switches off the television. Ramu goes to Dadiji and sits down on the floor beside her and softly says, "Dadiamma, Can I say something?" Dadiamma is still worried about her only grandson Nitin. She says, "Don't be so formal Ramu, speak what you want." Ramu in a low voice continues, "Dadiamma, for a few days I have noticed something! Nitin baba is somehow behaving differently than usually he does." Dadiji looks straight at Ramu and asks, "Why did he say anything to you? Ramu nods her head negatively and says that Nitin remains busy with his mobile always, and further says that he has noticed that whenever he enters into Nitin's room he always hides something from him, even Nitin has become very unmindful nowadays.

- You know Dadiji, I could see that Nitin Baba is not always with him. As if he is not here with us. Sometime it seems he belongs to anybody's else.

- What is it Ramu? Do you know what are you saying? Go and finish your kitchen work. Don't ever dare to say this type of stuff in front of Prabhu and Jaya. They'll teach you a lesson forever.Nitin is their only child.Nitin is their life.

Ramu sadly expresses, "But Dadiamma, I really love Nitin baba. I've taken care of him since he is in the cradle. I'm really concerned about him. In our village, I have seen such signs in them who are captured by ill spirits. Believe me Dadiamma, something wrong has happened to Nitin baba. Please do something. Save him from the ill spirit. "With tears running out of Ramu 's eyes, he goes to the kitchen.

Dadiji has anyhow stopped Ramu from further commenting on Nitin's behaviour. But Dadiji herself has noticed the Same thing with Nitin. Dadiamma is Nitin's favourite since the early days. Nitin's father Mr. Pravakar Gupta is the senior manager of a multinational company. He remains busy with his office work. Nitin's mother Jaya runs an NGO for the destitute. She also remains busy. From the tendered age Nitin has been habituated himself to live with his Dadiamma and Ramu. So any kind of change cannot be overlooked by Ramu.

Ramu was brought from an orphanage when Pravakar's dad passed away. He was brought as a companion to Mrs Subha Gupta, the Dadiji of Gupta Family. Since then Ramu has been a member of Gupta Family. After Nitin's birth, Nitin had a big brother and a sweet guardian in the guise of Ramu, a fourteen year old boy by then. With every passing day, Ramu Nitin and their Dadiamma developed a healthy friendship and an eternal bonding.

Tears come running fast as Dadiji recalls all these. She wonders how Nitin could be so indifferent towards his Daiamma and Ramu Bhaiya. Nitin shares every trivial matters to both of them. But for a month or two Nitin had changed himself to be noticed.

Just then the phone rings. Dadiji looks at the clock. It's eight o'clock now. With the worst thought Dadiji receives the call. Nitin's father is over the phone.

------ Ma, please give the phone to Nitin.

Pravu's voice startles Dadiji. Hesitatingly she replied, "But Pravu, Nitin has not come yet." In a much angry tone Pravu shouts over the phone, "What!! Didn't he say anything to you?" With a sigh and tears in her eyes Dadiji replied "No". The phone becomes silent. Dadiji feels the anger if Pravu because of Nitin. Nitin is not allowed to take his mobile phone when he is out for coaching classes. His final exams of B.COM are fast approaching. Dadiji is now crying profusely.

------Surely there is something wrong Ramu. Nitin must have done something terrific. Pravu is limitlessly angry with him. Where the he'll he is now? Why is he not coming to home?

The door bell rings. Ramu opens the door and Jaya enters with a cloudy face. Jaya is a beautiful lady with a beautiful dressing sense. But today there is no shine on her face. The natural glow has disappeared. Dadiji could easily realize that Jaya knows everything. But Dadiji is more concerned about Nitin's whereabouts. Ramu offers Jaya a glass of cold lemon water. After having g it Jaya sits down on the sofa beside Dadiji and asks

--------Maa, Had Nitin tell you anything about his activities nowadays?

Dadiji trembles.

-------Why beta? Is there anything wrong?

Jaya's voice softens. With a deep languish in her voice, Jaya says,

-------Maa, an amount of five thousand rupees is missing from Pravu's purse. Only we three knew about it. Last night Pravu kept it in his purse in front of Nitin. Nitin and I were discussing about the upcoming Diwali gift. Maa, What wrong is there that Nitin has to steal the money. He can't ask us.!!! Pravu is bitterly angry with Nitin. I don't have the least idea what is going to happen now.

Jaya is crying hysterically. Dadiji consoles her.

-----Don't get so tensed Beta. We will discuss the matter together with him. Now don't scold him away immediately. Try to behave normally as if nothing has happened.

Pravu enters with undefined anger. And with a loud call startles everyone,"NITIN......."

Nitin hasn't come yet. Dadiji starts praying to God to keep everything under control. She tries to pacify Pravu.

------ Please beta, calm down. You should not be so excited. Nitin is now a grown up boy. You should handle it with care.

Pravu breaks down like a child.

------What have we done??? Our only child has now learnt to steal money!!! Is this the day we are waiting for??

Dadiji is also in tears.

Dadiji pats on Pravu's shoulder.

------- Perhaps beta, there is a communication gap between Nitin and us, due to which he cannot pour his heart to us. Don't be so angry. First try to understand the situation. Let Nitin come. His late coming is bothering me. Where can he no now? It's almost ten at night.

Ramu has gone to look for Nitin, but comes back with a morose look. Jaya anxiously asks, "Have you seen him?"

------ No. There's a buzz in the market.

Pravu cries, "What's that? Speak out.

Ramu replied with downcast here, "Dadiamma, they say the boy who has been caught red handed pickpocketing in the shop looks almost like Nitin baba. Police has taken him with them.

Jaya faints instantly. Pravu remains seated like a statue. Dadiji breaks down on the sofa. Ramu begins to sprinkle water on Jaya's face. The gravity of the incident is such that no one in the house could speak to each other.

Just then the door bell rings. The family members are now dreading the worst. Perhaps the police has come with Nitin. Jaya starts moaning, "What will we say to our neighbours?". Dadiji orders Ramu to open the door.

Ramu with trembling happens the door only to find Nitin standing alone in a devastating state. He is not normal in his looks. As if he has come from a warfront. Ramu hugs him and pulls him into and closes the door. Jaya and Dadiji rush off to him and hug him. Jaya is in tears.

------ Where have you been Nitin? Couldn't you speak to your parents?

Nitin stands literally speechless. He could only manage to say, "Maa, there was no chance to ring back at home from the hospital."

-------HOSPITAL!!!!!

All of the members cry at once.

Dadiji controls the situation seeing that Nitin is about to break down in tears.

------ Go Nitin, get yourself refreshed. We are here to hear everything at the dinner.

-------But I have a lot to say Dadiamma.

-------We are also as much eager to know. But not in this way. Please get fresh first.

Nitin goes towards his room silently and slowly with his head down. Pravu is still furious.

------What will he say? He'll lie again.

Dadiji in a bit angry tone replies, "Please beta, don't be so silly. Nitin confessed that he has a lot to say. Let him speak first. We should give him a chance. Don't you notice that his appearance is not So normal.

-------But Maa, he has stolen. Can't you imagine the pregnancy of the crime???!!!

-------I really understand it beta, we should hold our patience. Please don't be so rude to Nitin without knowing everything. Try to understand what the situation demands. Nitin is in his last phase of teens, a very crucial transition. We all should handle him very sensitively. Remember, Your Papa never scolded you.

Nitin comes out at the dinning table and asks Ramu to serve the dinner. All the members are at the table. The dinner is ready to serve. Ramu is about to go to the kitchen. Nitin stops him,

-------"Ramu bhaiya please stand here. You should also know what have I done today?" Everybody is now speechless. Nitin is still in a pool of tears. Dadiji pats him. Nitin breaks down hysterically.

Jaya comes forward and hugs him, "What is the matter beta? Please speak up. Your silent tears are killing us."

Nitin controls himself and says, "Papa! I've taken five thousand rupees from your purse this morning without asking you.". Pravu is about to react. Dadiji stops him. Nitin goes on, "Maa, I've also taken an additional five thousand from your locker in the safe." Dadiji calmly says, "But Why Nitin? Why did you need that huge amount? "With utmost guilt Nitin continues irritatingly, "Dadiamma, I need that amount to deposit it in the LifeCare Nursing Home. You can contact them, there is my signature. I'm not lying Maa". Nitin turns to Jaya and both hug each other. Jaya softly asks him, "But why Nitin?"

Nitin remains silent. Pravu's anger has dropped a little. In a soft tone he asks, "Who was there in the nursing home?" Gathering courage Nitin speaks, "My friend Sarada." Now there is a pin drop silence. Nitin continues.

-------- I had done a wrong Maa. We love each other. Sarada is preparing for her class twelve exams.

We met through some common friends and come closer through Facebook and WhatsApp. Later we committed each other. It's since one year that we are seeing each other. Two months ago on a lonely evening while we were dating we lost our control.

Jaya and Pravu look at each other. Ramu goes towards the kitchen. Dadiji is sitting with her head down. Nobody has the courage to ask the next as it is clear now what are the dreadful chains of events. Nitin slowly continues.

-------They were not terminating the pregnancy unless the husband gives his consent. We approached most of the nursing homes. Sarada's close friend Ritu's maternal aunt is a gynaecologist.

Realizing everything she agrees at last. But the nursing home authority needs the signature of the husband. With no other option left, yesterday at the Ram-Sita Mandir we married each other. Today with the money, I took from you without your knowledge, I signed the consent paper as a husband; and they terminated............

Nitin is crying profusely. Everyone in the hall has become speechless. No One can hardly believe his ears. After a long pause Dadiji stands up. She hugged Nitin tightly. She is in tears. Jaya and Pravu are still sitting like statues. Nitin is still crying but goes on.

- Dadiamma it was an accident. Before we could understand anything, realize anything, the misfortune overlapped us. But we really love each other Dadiamma. We repent for it. We have no way because we like to concentrate on our career. We care for our family also. We respect our family image. We've decided not to meet again until we both are established in our respective fields. We'll only talk over phone.

Dadiji sighs, "But Nitin you have killed....."

Nitin stops Dadiji and exclaims, "Dadiamma it was my responsibility. How can I avoid my role in this. I could not avoid all these and leave Sarada in this state to fight alone. My conscience prevented me. Sarada lives here as a PG. Her parents are unaware of the fact. She completely relies on me. How can I leave her all by herself? I've seen my parents take care of each other so tenderly. I've always seen you and Ramu bhaiya respecting the family values. I have to take the step. Please forgive me."

Dadiji has no words to say anything. Nitin turns towards Pravu and says, "Papa, forgive me. I should have tell you and Maa about all these. But I was afraid. I feared to loose Sarada. Please forgive me Maa. I could not respect your morality. I even couldn't respect a girl's chastity. But I repent it. I really feel sorry for what I have done."

Now Pravu reacts.

------ Enough is enough Nitin. What do you think? We'll give you an adorable hug and welcome you. We'll admire your decision taking ability!!! What do you think of us?

Jaya and Dadiji both stand holding each other undecided. Jaya softly says

------ Nitin, Now go to your room. It's tiresome now. Give us the space of our own.

Nitin slowly stands up and moves forward to his room. He is to step inside. Pravu calls him. Nitin turns around. Pravu with a fatherly affection proclaims,

------ Bring my Bahu tomorrow at our house. We will talk to her and her parents. They shouldn't be kept in dark. But we should also remember that she is rightfully the daughter-in-law of this family. Now go and take rest. Tell her to be prepared to come to her in-laws tomorrow. And your mom will be her local guardian till she gets married.

Nitin rushes to Pravu and hugs him tightly. Dadiji and Jaya also join them. Ramu prays silently with a smile on his face. Dadiji breathes a sigh of relief.

THE WAR WITHIN

Neha is getting ready. Mummiji enters and asks, "Are you getting ready Beta?" Neha casually answers the positive. Then with a pause and in an anxious tone asks, "Mummiji, do you think I should take Sonu with me?" Without any hesitation and dreading the worst Mummiji discards Neha's proposal and just casually says, "You just go and bring our son. It's since six months we are going through the pain of this separation. And I 've already told Sonu that his dad is coming back from an office tour of abroad. He and I will be making preparation for our darling dad and we laughed a lot on this yesterday evening. Though Sonu is not at the age to realize all these but we had a talk last evening". Neha is much tensed today. Again she asks

-----Will it be all over Mummiji?

In a convincing tone Mummiji replies, "Of course. Have faith. There's nothing impossible."

-----Is Papaji coming with me today, Mummiji?

Mummiji interrupts Neha in the middle and firmly says, "Do as I say. Go alone. Once you two are at home, everything'll be fine. It's my intuition and belief also.. Now hurry up and bring back my Sudhir. Don't get late. You have to travel a long distance."

Neha hurries up. Just then their driver Pushkar comes and confirms that everything is ready and they can start at once. Mummiji in an affectionate tone says Pushkar,

------ Listen Beta, drive carefully and pay full attention. Don't stop to talk with anyone known or unknown. The windows should be pulled over.

Pushkar assures Mummiji about Neha's security and Sudhir's safe arrival at home. Mummiji pats Pushkar on his head and in a blissful tone asserts,

-----I know I can completely rely on you. You're your father's favourite. You also know this very well. Your Sudhir Bhaiya also depends on you more than his own blood.

Pushkar happily agrees and goes out to reach the car. Neha hugs Mummiji and asks for Papaji.

Mummiji nods her head negatively.

- No Beta, he's not well you know. You start your journey. I'll manage here.

Neha hugs and kisses Sonu and hands him over to Mummiji. Neha thinks that perhaps Sonu is asking for his father. Neha's eyes become moist. She adores her baby and assures that she will surely bring back his father to him by the evening.

Neha is waiting in front of the billing counter. Neha gives a big sigh to see that her token number is 28 where the processing number of the token is only 10. Still a long time to wait, Neha says in her mind. All these six months she is visiting here on the weekends secretly as if some wrong doings are going on. She's the only witness how Sudhir, her dear husband, started responding to the treatment and goes through the process like an obedient student with not a single scope of any grievances or allegations on any side. Neha has silently watched Sudhir without being noticed by him. Tears roll up her eyes. She is just to wipe it out suddenly she fills pat on her right shoulder. She startles and looks aside only to find her bestie Nirmala standing beside her. Neha becomes speechless firstly for this

unexpected meeting after such a long time and secondly, she feels that she has been caught red handed. An unknown fear embraces her. Nirmala is also much happy to see her. Overcoming the initial tension Neha only manages, "Nirmala!!!" The person on the other side is so much happy to meet her pal after such a long period that she hugs her tightly as they frequently did in their college days. When both of them have overcome the suddenness of the situation they choose a farthest corner to sit and have a chat with each other.

Nirmala has joined as a consultant in this institute only two months back. And what a coincidence for Neha to hear that Nirmala has been assisting Sudhir's doctor Mr. Pravakar since then without knowing the fact that Sudhir is her best Pal's dear husband. Neha realizes that nothing is secret to Nirmala now. Suppressing any kind of fact or even trying to do such an act May worsen the matter.

Neha feels somehow shattered. She does not know how to manage this sudden outcome. The secret, which had been kept a secret only among four of them, has been unveiled to Nirmala.!!! Even Nirmala has not exposed much to her parents. Neha dives deep into the ocean of thought when Nirmala gives her a shake, "Hey! I know you all are trying to keep Sudhir's illness a secret from the rest of the world for his shake and may be to avoid social harassment. While assisting Dr Pravakar, I had to go through Sudhir's case history and since then I knew that his wife visits regularly at the weekend. But I never could imagine that the very person might be you. Only a few weeks ago I learned it. But I didn't get the courage to meet you."

Neha eyes get moist. She softly asks, "Do you know everything? I mean the reason behind Sudhir's illness !!!"

------ Partially. But how did it all happen?

Neha breaks down, "It's all have to be. This is what we call destiny."

Just then the ward boy hangs up the LUNCH BREAK board. It means that the bill clearance slip is to be despatched after the break. Nirmala notices this and offers Neha to have a cup of coffee. Neha agrees with no choice left. Ordering two cups of coffee for them these two childhood friends arrange a corner table for themselves and make themselves ready for a chat.

Neha goes on saying, "You know Nirmala I've made myself dumb in front of my all relatives and friends during all these six months. Today I'll pour my all heart to you. Because it's getting difficult for me to hold further." Neha hysterically breaks down. Nirmala tries to make Neha calm down.

------- Neha, Your fight has just started. Be strong enough. What were you doing since six months

were confined up to you. Now you have to be with Sudhir not only virtually, but literally.

-------Nirmala, let me open up myself to you. All these days I've been living like a corpse.

Nirmala, with a motherly affection, pacified Neha. Neha goes on,

------- We're happily married for two years, and planning for a baby. At the end of the second year, something uncanny we felt. We consulted the popular gynaecologists of the city. I underwent all tests, no stones remained unturned. But All my reports were normal, rather extremely fine according to my doctors.

------Very good.

------No it's not that good. Doctors suggested Sudhir to go through some tests. Sudhir did

accordingly and those tests confirmed that Sudhir is incapable.

------ Wait! Sudhir's case history shows that he is the father.....

------ Yes, we have a son.

------- Okay. Then what happened? Didn't your in-laws comment anything ?

-------Nirmala, my in-laws are very supportive and they are very open minded. They accepted the fact. They never let me down, and even stood by Sudhri. They also asserted that if we're deprived of any heir, we should not worry. But we should live happily with each other.

-------It's great to have such supportive in-laws.

-------Yes, I'm fortunate enough. But the problem was elsewhere. Sudhir could not accept the fact.

He became irritable and started coming late at home. Mummiji explained a lot to Sudhir, but all in vain. Then we decided to go for an adoption. But again Sudhir refused. It was a very tough time for me. On one hand there was the pain of not being able to be a mother, and on the other I had to handle Sudhir with care. Then one day my gynaecologist suggested that we could take the help of sperm donor. She gave us the necessary contacts.

------ That's very interesting!!!!

------ Yeah!!! Sudhir agreed. And after three months of tireless effort good news was in the air.

I conceived and doctors council Sudhir that he had also fathered the foetus. I didn't know how but it worked. Sudhir was back to normal life. We were happy again and time took us to the seventh heaven when after nine months Sony was born. Our family was complete.

------Then all these?????

------Sonu's first birthday celebration was a grand celebration. Relatives and friends came. A long awaited get together was that. That night still lingers in my mind. We were all very tired. I was busy putting Sonu to sleep. Suddenly Sudhir asked, "Who might be the father of Sonu?" Believe me Nirmala, I couldn't trust my ears. Words fell short for any expression. Still I put on a smile on my face, controlled my tears and managed to say, "What a joke Sudhir!!! You're Sonu's one and only father." Sudhir remained indifferent to my answer. Rather he replied "No, no, I mean whose sperm is there....." I couldn't take it anymore Nirmala and outrageously reacted, "Stop it Sudhir!" Sudhir left the room instantly and I was devastated.

--------Oh!!! I could understand Sudhir's psychological ups and downs.

---------May Be! But again my family was at a stake. It was Sudhir's iron determination that he must find out the truth. He frequently reduced his office and went in search of the real donor.

--------- That's very ridiculous. Didn't you stop?

---------- How could I? He stopped sharing anything with me. Only then we could realize that he has bunked his office when he returns early at home. Mummiji, Papaji both tried to make out some solutions, they even talked to Sudhir, but nothing worked. Then one day Sudhir came home in a dilapidated condition. We were frightened to see that face of Sudhir. Sudhir was dangerously silent. Not a single word did he utter. He was normal in his outward dealings—he took dinner, he changed and refreshed himself but without uttering a single sound. Next day he was more silent. Not in a mood to go to his office and made himself confined to bed.

--------Didn't you ask anything? Didn't you even try to make him speak?

-------- A thousand times. But no answer. Even no expression. It seemed that we were pouring words into deaf ears. This went on for two days. Suddenly one morning he locked himself in the room, when I was busy with Sonu in the washroom. We were clueless about this. The suddenness of the situation startled us. We called our driver Pushkar. He broke the lock of the door only to find Sudhir lying unconscious. He was immediately shifted to the nearby nursing home where he was diagnosed with severe mental trauma.

--------- Didn't you try to find the cause even after all these happened?

---------- We did. And that was truly shocking. We had no ground under our feet.

---------- What does it mean?

----------Sudhir was discharged from the nursing home. Then he was shifted to your institute. After he was shifted here, doctors suggested for a continuous stay for six months in this institute for his speedy and permanent recovery. The cost was also affordable for us. We agreed. After everything were finalized we frantically searched for the reason at home. We ransacked his locker, his office bag, files and every possible corners; and at last found the real cause of our sufferings.

-------And what was that?

-------The Donor!!!!!!

Neha is in pool of tears. Nirmala senses the complication and pacified Neha, "Leave it here. No need to discuss it."

-------Nirmala, that Almighty has other plans for us. Where our thoughts and plans end, HIS starts; and this happened with us. Wouldn't you like to hear who the donor is?

Nirmala has already sensed the complexity and the gravity of the situation. She tries to avoid it, but Neha again breaks down.

----Okay Neha, speak up. Tell me everything. I promise I'll be there always with you and for you.

-----Nirmala, he's none other than my father-in-law, my Papaji.

------WHAT?!!!!!!

Nirmala becomes speechless. She even forgets to blink her eyes. She manages herself and then answers with great difficulty, "Are you sure?"

------ Yes, Nirmala. The reports in Sudhir's file confirmed the truth.

------- And your Papaji?

------- That night we brought the papers in front of him. He looked at the papers like a baby boy being caught by mother while doing some naughty assignments. Then he howled and cried and said, "I didn't think such a day will ever come". Then he narrated the whole incident. Here is his version.

"It wad almost six years back. Sudhir had been enrolled in the MBA programme after completing his engineering. Though the admission was done on the education loan, other expenses were there also. The expense was dreading me. Your Mummiji and I were 18 and 21 years old respectively when we got married. After graduation I joined my father's garment business and married and within two years of our marriage we had lost our first child also. So when Sudhir came in our life we decided to provide everything for Sudhir's better prospect. The more I tried to improve my business with the latest technology, the higher the cost of living increased. The profit from my business was not enough. Day by day it was becoming more difficult for me. On one end there was regular investments in the business, household expenses, rituals, social obligations and on the other end, there were the cost of Sudhir's pocket money, hostel expenses, fooding and everything. The business was also in recession. I was left with no other option than to search for a part time job for some extra income. Before opening the shop at eleven in the morning, I started working as a data entry operator for a private firm in the morning shift on contractual basis. While working on the computer, once I came across the job of Sperm Donor. They were offering a good salary. I thought a lot. But necessity and obligation is something that can't be ignored. My necessity won over my hesitation and I applied. As my age was forty-seven, I had to go through some tests apart from those normal and general tests abide by their rules and regulations. I never had the idea that I would get selected. But it happened and the handsome salary meet my every ends for those two years. After Sudhir got recruited with a prestigious salary I opted out myself from all those part time jobs. And that job of donor ship remained a secret within me. Even your Mummiji was in dark about all these till today until my own son has gone through this. Ohh!!! What an irony!!!

There was a long pause. Nirmala couldn't utter a single word. Suddenly Neha notices the time and hurries up to the billing counter. Yes, the next number is hers. She stands in the queue. Now she feels very light and relieved from within. She says to herself, "Perhaps I've disobeyed my mother-in-law, but I think I need this. Otherwise this reticence was killing me. Don't know what Nirmala is thinking Now! But she should say something to me. I really need her clinical advise! Not as a friend, but as a doctor." The billing counter announces her name. Neha pays all the fuss and everything is done smiithlt and systematically.

Neha is about to enter Sudhir's cabin, just then Nirmala stops her. Neha is surprised to see her at this time. Nirmala takes Neha aside,

------- Don't even speak to anybody about our conversation, no need to reveal that we are friend and well acquainted to each other. And listen.....

------ I know Nirmala, but I think I need counselling. To go to Sudhir, to face him, to talk to him seem impossible now. I'm trembling from within. May be I am lacking the courage.

------ Don't worry. You first overcome your fear and be normal as if nothing has happened. And call me at any time when you feel. But call me Dr. Nirmala in front of anybody else. I'll be there always for you. (Nirmala hugs Neha.)

After a pause of a second or two Nirmala says,

------Neha, I think you three should shift to a separate house. This is the demand of this situation. You should move with your son and husband before any embarrassing situation engulfs you.

------What're you saying? Where shall we go? Sudhir is on without pay for these months. His office knows that he has gone to Mumbai for his cousin brother's treatment. My Papaji sister's only son is really fighting for life due to lungs cancer. But is stable now as it was in the initial stage when the disease was detected. We took that advantage of the situation for our sake. You know Neha we have also booked false tickets to entrust his office.

------- I can understand everything. But it would be helpful if Sudhir gets some time more to face his dear Dad. It's just a few months that he has come across such a burning truth. I personally think this.Take your time. You say your in-laws are very supportive. Talk to them. Ask them about it, do it accordingly.

------- Thanks Nirmala.

Neha enters Sudhir's cabin. The ward boy has made everything ready. Seeing Neha the ward boy leaves to bring the discharge file and the list of medicines. Neha hugs Sudhir and her eyes are filled with tears. Sudhir hugs Neha tightly. Neha feels thrilled. She could feel that same secured touch that she has been missing since a year. Sudhir smiles and softly says,

------- Now I'm okay dear. Everything'll be alright. I'll make things like before. Now let's go home. I'm eager to see my son, my parents. We'll be happy together.

Neha couldn't believe her ears. She wipes her tears away and gives a call to Pushkar. He comes and also breaks down in tears out of joy to see his Sudhir Bhaiya is absolutely fine.

Within three hours they are at home. Neha feels relieved to see that Sudhir is playing with Sonu like a normal loving father. Even he is talking with his Dad normally. And Papaji is also normal with Sudhir. They are chating with each other. The whole family is in happy mood. Neha is preparing some delicacies of Sudhir's choice. Mummiji is helping her. Neha softly says,

------ Mummiji, how relieved it feels to see our dear ones happy again. May God bless our family and us!!"

Mummiji smiles and nods her head. Then she comes close to Neha and gives her a bunch of keys and says,

------- Neha, all these are the keys of my bedroom, my bank lockers, my safe, my cupboard. There is a file in my safe where there are important documents of house and bank. Keep these all in your safety. We're going away tomorrow early in the morning.

Neha stands speechless.

-------Tomorrow morning? Sudhir and Pushkar are also going for two days to Mumbai you know. Sudhir is supposed to submit those used tickets to rejoin at office. How can l live without you all?

-------No Neha, They're not going. We're going only. That is, me and your Papaji. We 're going to live with Vasudha. She needs us. After her husband's death her son was her only support to live. But now that is too at a stake. So we've decided to live with her. Moreover, Sudhir is your responsibility now. You should be his mentor and guide in every possible ways. And I know that you will prove to be an ideal wife. We are always with you. You can call us at any time. We'll come once in a year and you can also visit us.

------That means you all are leaving us for ever. And all for your son's wellbeing? Don't I mean anything to you?

-------Beta, Sudhir is my son. But Papaji is my husband, my everything. The irony has left him no where. As you stand by your husband, now I've to do the same.

Your Papaji needs a break. May be I also need it. And Vasudha's and our situation are complementary to each other. This is the irony of life. If that Almighty wants, we'll live together again. Don't worry. Pushkar is like Lakshmana to Sudhir. He'll take good care of you all.

They hug each other. Pain in voice and tears in eyes both feel the warmth in each other's cosiness. Mummiji sighs, "Neha, you have fought your battle and on the way to win. My battle is going to begin from tomorrow. As a mother I have fought it. As a wife it is just to begin. May God bless us all!!"

FINALLY...

"What happened Dear?! You look so depressed. Anything wrong? Any health problem?", a thoughtful Rimi asks these questions to her bestie Ritu anxiously. Today Ritu is not in her normal mood. Rimi righteously feels something is wrong with Ritu that she is hiding or trying to express in her own way.

Ritu tries to open her up to Rimi only by a long sigh. Just then the smart phone starts ringing from her purse. Rimi hurriedly takes out the phone, sees who's calling and receives the call with the speaker on. Ritu could easily stop her, but some unknown reason prevents her from this and let Rimi do whatever she wants.

Now the speaker on the other side starts roaring, "Aree Mummiji when are you coming? Don't you know Ritesh has an important meeting to attend in the office? I have to ready Bittu with his preparation for the unit test. Now who'll do the kitchen? Is Ritesh to starve today or you think I am to do with all these?" Rimi becomes furious and is about to reply. Ritu stops her and answers, "Coming Beta, just 10 minutes. I'm on the way." From the other side it's heard, "Please do come and do us a favour. We are just disturbed with this daily drama you know". The phone becomes silent.

Ritu is in tears. She busily starts for home. Rimi stops her, "What are you doing Ritu? Is this what you deserve? What's wrong with you? Why are you bearing all these?" Ritu replies in a broken voice, "Let me leave now Rimi. Tomorrow We'll discuss about it" and does not wait.

Rimi and Ritu, both in their mid-sixties, are best friend from their college life. Even after their marriage they were in close contact. After retiring from the post of Deputy Commissioner, Mr. Shekhar Sinha, the loving and caring husband of Ritu gifted her a two storied huge magnificent bungalow with a decorated garden. Ritu was overwhelmed. Their only son Ritesh was studying engineering at a prestigious college in Chennai. So with no worries for Ritesh's career and with a handsome pension of Shekhar, Ritu and Shekhar moved to this magnificent palace like bungalow at Bangalore. The superannuation of Shekhar seemed glorious with a loving wife at their heavenly abode. One day Rimi called Ritu to give the good news of their shifting to Bangalore also and on an evening walk they happened to meet. Rimi and Prakash both were also enjoying their superannuation after retiring from the post of Assistant Professor at government colleges and running an NGO for the abandoned parents and children. The friendship between these two couples flourished and nourished within no time. It seemed they were in the seventh heaven.

The second phase of Shekhar's superannuation started with his prolonged illness caused due to cerebral attack. Meanwhile Ritesh got posted as project manager with a reputed MNC and fortunately in Bangalore. With no hope of recovery, Shekhar confined himself in the room. Ritu decided to get her son married with girl he was seeing since his college days. As decided Ritesh got married to Shraddha and within one year Ritu and Shekhar had a lovely grandson. But two years back Shekhar passed away leaving his family under the loving care of Ritu.

"Beta come here. I've served your breakfast". Ritu calls Ritesh affectionately. Ritesh takes his seat at the table and sighed, "Oh! No. This puri-sabzi has no alteration Mamma." Ritu smiles and says, "There's on bread so that I can't prepare your favourite sandwiches. But I've prepared some besan laddoo. Will you have them?" Ritesh agrees. Ritu brings them from the kitchen and serves them to Ritesh. Ritesh hesitatingly asks, "Mamma is it mandatory for you to go for the Puja in the morning daily?" Ritu surprisingly asks, "Why Beta?" Just then Shraddha pours in, "Why Mummiji? We've a big Puja ghar. Is it not enough to worship there?" Ritu stammers surprisingly. Not knowing what to answer Ritu tries to be bold, "No, this isn't possible. I'll go and it's sure". Ritu disappears into the kitchen. Shraddha and Ritesh are totally surprised at such boldness and could not utter a single word. Ritu silently serves the breakfast for Shraddha and Bittu with tears in her eyes which her son or daughter-in-law couldn't see or feel. Bittu comes and hugs his granny from behind that melts the ice. Ritu hugs her grandson and kisses frantically to wipe her tears. Bittu could've felt something and cries loudly, "Mamma, look granny is crying. You must have scold my granny. She works a lot. You still scold her." Ritu immediately stops Bittu by putting a laddoo in his mouth. Shraddha is about to say something but Ritesh stops her. Shraddha takes both her and son's dishes and walks into the bedroom with Bittu scolding him, "Come on Bittu. You're getting late for school and also ill-mannered day by day." Bittu unwillingly follows his mother.

Ritesh bids goodbye to Shraddha and Bittu for office. He asks Ritu to lock the main door. Ritu comes quickly and pats on Ritesh's shoulder who has bent down to put on the shocks. Just before leaving, Ritesh hugs his Mom and gently says, "Please, Mamma take care of all and don t try to tell us something through Bittu. He is much young to understand politics. Please don't use him", and Ritesh leaves without giving even a small scope to justify herself. Ritu's tears come rolling down from her eyes. She locks the door and slowly walks into her bedroom. She lits an incense stick and stares steadily at Shekhar's photo. Tears come fast from her eyes. But neither weeps nor she sighs. Just then from outside, "Mummiji we're leaving. I'll be back at 2.30 with Bittu. Hope by then you'll do away with those cooking and washing. We'll have lunch together with

Bittu beta". Bittu feels very exciting. He kisses his grandma and leaves for school.

It's now 3 p.m. Ritesh comes out from the conference hall and he is much happy. The meeting is successful and it means another project with a promotion and salary hike and everything is finalized. He opens the phone from his pocket to call his darling wife just then the phone rings. Ritesh gets excited to see "Shraddha Calling". He receives the call in no time and with out asking anything he outbursts, "Shraddha, tell Mom this good news. We'll celebrate at night." From the other side Shraddha cries aloud, "Whom to tell Ritesh? Where's your Mom? I've returned with Bittu almost had an hour ago. She's not in the house. Even she left her phone on the dinning table. Now I've to clean up Bittu and myself, then only can we eat. What happen? Now speak up. What to celebrate? Your success or you Mother's playful mood?" Ritesh is in no mood to get disturbed, "Oh no Shraddha! Don't be so bitter today. A very glorious time is fast approaching for us. Now darling, go and serve yourself and Bittu the lunch. Don't worry Mom will return within a while. Ritesh feels that Shraddha has dropped the call. But Ritesh becomes restless. He starts having his Tiffin at the office canteen but his mind fearfully awaits Shraddha's next call that will confirm his mom's come back. May be it will not be a good interaction for anybody, still Ritesh awaits the call. But hours pass without a call from

Shraddha. Ritesh gets busy meanwhile. Suddenly he happens to look at his wristwatch and notices that it is 5 o'clock. Ritesh senses that his Mom has surely come back and that's why Shraddha hasn't call him. With a sense of relief Ritesh rings his Mom. But the phone goes on ringing, nobody answers his call, neither first time nor the second time. Ritesh, getting tensed, calls Shraddha. The same here. No answers from Shraddha despite repetitive calls from Ritesh. With a sigh Ritesh sits down. After sometime Shraddha calls Ritesh only to inform him that she is on a hang out with friends at the city mall and Bittu is also with her. Ritesh is to ask about his mother but

till then Shraddha has cut the call, and Ritesh is left with no clues of his Mom. Just then the idea of calling Rimi aunty occurs to Ritesh In no time Ritesh rings her. Rimi takes the call and an excited Ritesh, without any formality, asks, "Aunty, is Mamma there at your place?" Rimi, with her usual calmness, answers, "Yes beta, she came here in the afternoon; and left for home an hour ago. She is about to reach. Don't worry." Ritesh gets relieved, "Thank you Aunty. Actually Mom has left her phone behind and I was much worried. She has never gone anywhere without informing, this is for the first time...." ; Rimi stops Ritesh in the middle and assures him, "Don't worry. Your mom is a strong person. She can handle every situation. You know one thing Ritesh, the day your Mom started learning to live without her husband, she started learning to live alone, all by herself. Go home." Rimi stops the phone. Ritesh becomes surprised.

It is 6 o'clock in the morning. Ritu has taken bath already like any other day. But today she has decided not to go for the Morning Prayer. Instead she will call Rimi at her residence for some important discussions once Shraddha and Bittu leave for school. Ritu comes out of her room to prepare the morning breakfast and to her utter surprise she finds a busy Shraddha in the kitchen preparing breakfast and morning tea.Ritu hurries up with the utensils so that it can help Shraddha to serve quickly. Shraddha adorably asks, "Mummiji, have you done with your Puja?" Ritu politely answers, "Yes, beta." Shraddha in the same tone asks, "Then serve your plate also. Today we'll have our breakfast together." Ritu doesn't protest and serves her plate; but her heart knows that too much politeness from the other side is the onset of a devastating torpedo. But Ritu consoles herself, "No Ritu, not anymore; this time you have to be bold enough to speak." Ritesh has made Bittu ready for school. They both come to the table and the family sits for breakfast together after a long time. Tears are in Ritu's eyes. She recalls those glorious days spent with Shekhar. Shraddha serves sandwiches and fruit juice, there are also those besan laddoo that Ritu prepared yesterday.

Amazing silence is casted on as their breakfast goes on. Ritesh breaks off the silence and in a merry tone says, "Mamma, I've got a good news for you. Yesterday I've signed another prestigious project Mamma. I'm so happy. This project is a collaboration with a foreign company. They're visiting India." Ritu feels too contended. She, with a satisfying smile on her lips, blessed her son, "God bless you Ritesh. Your Dad and I had always wanted your progress. I'm so happy Beta." Ritesh excitedly says, "Mamma, this is a two year project and may extend up to five years. My company will be providing me a luxurious fully furnished two-thousand square feet flat with all modern amenities along with a handsome salary this time." Ritu indifferently nods this time as if what is going to happen is already known to her. Ritesh partially could read his mom's reaction. He thoughtfully answers, "Mamma, but there's a problem." Ritu instantly puts a glance on Shraddha and then in an assuring tone says, "What's the problem? You've to shift to other city, right? And you're going to take your wife and son with you. There's nothing wrong in it. Go ahead. Your career should be your priority. Now tell me which city?" Ritesh slowly answers, "It's Mumbai Mamma." Ritu joyfully reacts, "That's great. The city of magic!" Ritu then changes her tone and boldly says, "You first go there Ritesh, get everything arranged and obviously a maid first on whole time basis to prepare your breakfast, lunch and dinner according to all of your choices, to do with the utensils then, to wash your clothes and for every household works. Then only take your wife and son, because in your new luxurious flat there will be no Mamma." Ritu smiles and goes to the kitchen with her dish. Shraddha roughly attacks Ritesh, "Look at her, she does not leave any chance to hurt me. This is such a joyous news and Mummiji is creating a mess unnecessary." Ritesh becomes dumb.

Shraddha just wants to say something, but Ritesh stops her, "Please Shraddha, stop now. Everything is in your favour. Now spare that old woman."

It's now almost eleven o'clock. Ritu comes downstairs. She doubts whether Ritesh and Shraddha are sleeping, but thankfully sees that the lights are on in their bedroom. Though urgent, Ritu hesitates to knock. Tomorrow morning they'll be leaving for Mumbai; only few hours left. Two months passed since Ritesh had told about his promotion, his shifting to a new city. Ritu wonders how time flies. "Will it be okay to call them at this hour?" hesitatingly Ritu walks about and opens the door of the kitchen to fetch a glass of water. Just then Ritesh comes out of his room and gets surprised to see Ritu till awake at this late hour He asks, "Mamma, you at this time?" Ritu smartly answers, "Yes, I've to give you something. Call Shraddha also." At that very moment Shraddha comes out hearing the commotion from her bedroom. Ritu continues, "I've very important task to complete." Both Ritesh and Shraddha look at each other with much suspense. Ritu gives a file and a bag to Ritesh and politely says, "These all are for you. You may consider it as your parting gift from Mamma." Ritesh becomes standstill and asks, "What do you mean by parting gift Mamma?" Ritu in that same polite tone says, "Go through the papers in the file and open the bag. You'll understand everything." Ritesh opens the file while Shraddha the bag. Out of surprise they forget to utter a single word. Ritu explains, "Look, there're some jewellery which I got as a gift from my parents and in-laws during my marriage. Now they all belong to Bittu's wife that means my grand daughter-in-law. It's the reality of life that when Bittu will attain the age of marriage I'll be not here in the world to bless the couple. So give them to her as a blessing from me and your Dad and all our ancestors. Here are the papers which prove that Bittu and his wife will inherit them; till then Shraddha will be the legal care taker of these jewels". Ritesh gets disturbed, "Is it necessary to do all these? Why Mamma? This's much annoying to me you know!" Just then his eyes become still once again. With much wonder he cries, "What's here? A cheque of rupees fifty lacs!" Shraddha quickly glances at the cheque. Ritu smiles," Don't be so impatient. Let me explain first."

Ritu sits on a chair at the dining table. She rubs her specs with the end part of her Saree and then putting them on, she continues with a sigh,

"You remember that day, two months ago, when I was off for the whole day without intimating you anything; and then you returned home and the next day you conveyed me the good news of your promotion. This chapter started that very day. I was just getting tired of all those household turmoil between you and me. That afternoon, after preparing the meal, I decided to visit your Rimi Aunty at her office. I was on the way where at the bus Stand I happened to meet your office colleague Sanjib Desai. He came once on Bittu's birthday. So he was not unknown to me. He came to me and asked me about my well being and very earnestly asks, "Aunty, next time when I'll be in Mumbai, I'll come to your new home and have those barfis prepared by You." I was too surprised to speak. Desai went on saying a lot but nothing could I hear. After sometime I recovered myself and answered, "No Beta, I'm not going to Mumbai, I'll be here in that Bungalow which is my husband's gift to me and you can easily come to me for those barfis." Desai, with an unhappy expression said, "But Ritesh would feel very disappointed Aunty. He submitted a list of his family members yesterday to ensure a big flat of two thousand square feet in Mumbai. I was there at the meeting and I saw Ritesh handing over the list to our boss.

Meanwhile the bus came. I boarded it and bade goodbye to Desai. Sitting in the bus I thought about myself. The wife in me died on that very day when your Papa passed away. I was from then only your mother, Shraddha's Mummiji and Bittu's grandma. But somehow I felt I would loose my identity in near future. I went to Rimi's NGO. She was there and seeing her I broke down in front of her out of the fear of being left alone and looking you. Rimi consoled me and I asked her to give me a new identity so that I can live by myself, because by then I had the clear picture that you guys are leaving Bangalore for sure.

Rimi and her husband had no children biologically. Rimi took me inside the NGO House and pointed all those children who were living without anybody of their own. Rimi had become their Amma. I exclaimed with joy, "It's so sweet Rimi". Rimi merrily agrees and says, "Isn't it? I love to be with them." After a pause Rimi asks, "Ritu why can't you become their grandma?" I was shocked initially. Gradually I could catch Rimi's words and I gave her my word.

While all these are going on, Rimi's husband Prakash called and I felt from their conversation that they were in a tension to accommodate twenty children. I hurried to get out from there. But Rimi stopped me and asked me to stay the whole day with them. A gala time was spent with those little innocent angels. I returned home;

and there was an abnormal silence which I knew would turn into a devastating torpedo;---- the very next day you told me that you are going to shift to Mumbai with your family, and your family does not include me. Believe me or not, the mother, mother-in-law and the grandmother all these three died at once at that very moment. Finishing the breakfast that Shraddha serves that day I went to my room, cried without limits and instantly decided to donate the ground floor of this bungalow to house those twenty helpless children. I called Rimi to settle everything. But Rimi advised me to sell the ground floor property and give the money to you as a share of your Dad's property. I considered it as a wise decision and did everything accordingly. Here are these papers which show everything are legally done and now on you and your family have no right or share on this property. No need to look back. Go ahead."

Ritu goes slowly but steadily to her room in the upper storey. Ritesh and Shraddha remain dumb and motionless.

TO BE DESTINED

After a long gap of fifteen years Nidhi is going to meet her bestie Sudha. They have fixed an appointment at 12 noon in this cafeteria at the centre of the city. But Nidhi

couldn't control her emotions and has arrived an hour before. She just does not want Sudha to wait for her.

Arriving at the cafeteria she orders a cup of tea, picks up a weekly magazine from the book-corner and makes her comfortable at the booked seat. She looks at the mirror and eyes her greyish locks that are indicative of passing of time so swiftly. She smiles all by herself," So what! My mind is still at sixteen!" With the word sixteen, some old memories flashes in her mind. It was the 16th of August that she and Sudha met for the first time at the Principal's room when they were about to start their teaching career as Assistant Mistress in a renowned school in Kolkata. It was their joining date. Both were brimming with new excitement and promises. Principal Madam Mrs. Bhatia introduced them to each other and a promising friendship instantly struck between Nidhi Gupta, an M.A in History, from a middle class family with down-to -earth personality and Sudha Mishra, an M.Sc in Zoology, from a high-profile family with high ambition. Though they are at two poles from outward dimensions, there's a common line between them and that's their positivity and bubbliness and,of course, their age. Their basic differences towards life never came in their relation. Rather they compliment each other.

Nidhi's thoughts are disturbed by the Waiter's sudden offering, "Ma'am your tea! Anything else?" Nidhi looks at him and nods negatively," Thank you." As soon as the waiter departs, Nidhi takes a glance at her watch and says to herself," There's half an hour to go; I wonder my mind is going faster or the clock is slower today" and again smiles and engages herself in recalling those sweet memories spent with Sudha.

Some indignant sounds of reckless laughing, greetings and cheering now and then intersects the rhythm of the act of reminiscing. Nidhi takes a glance at the far corner from where those sounds are coming. There is a celebration going on and for sure, it is an anniversary celebration. The candle in the middle boastfully proclaims that it's a fifth year celebration. "Ah! What a coincidence!", Nidhi says to herself with wide- opening eyes. A same scenario comes in her mind ringing the happy tune that was played as a background music when Sudha cut their fifth anniversary cake. It was an intimate get together arranged with only family members and close friends. Nidhi was truly amazed when Sudha called her the previous night. Those words

are still in the air," Nidhi Dear! What are you doing?".
Nidhi's married life was then only a month old. She
was dutifully busy with her mom-in-law at the kitchen
preparing the dinner just after returning from school.
Nidhi merrily answered," Helping Mummiji. But at
this time, anything serious? "Sudha most excitedly
replied, "No Dear, tomorrow is my fifth anniversary.
We have arranged a small party at the country club.
Please do come with Arun Bhaiya. You know just my
closer pals." Nidhi happily agrees but at the same time
felt much surprised to find herself in the closer list
of Sudha's pals. An eternal bonding stabilized more
dominatingly.

Nidhi looks at her watch. It's almost twelve. Her
heart starts beating loudly. Feeling thrilled Nidhi asks
herself, "What's happening with me! "Her inquiry
is interrupted by the smart ringtone. She hurriedly
reaches it thinking Sudha. But oh no!!! She receives
the call, "Yes Beta, I've reached. No no it's okay. No
your Sudha Aunty hasn't turned up yet. I'm your
mother and a responsible person Beta. Please don't
get tensed. I'll take a cab. There's no need to send the
driver. Okay bye." Nidhi says all these at a stretch and
ends the call. She smiles all by herself again, "What a
daughter I have! At the age of sixty- five, she calls me
CHILD!!" Just then an app cab parks in front of the
cafe gate. Nidhi 's intuition righteously guesses, "Yes,
it's Sudha!" And Lo! Sudha comes out of the cab and

enters through the gate. Nidhi raises her hand to help Sudha locate Nidhi easily. Nidhi recalls the day when they met for the last time before fifteen years. Sudha's husband Raju had to settle in Mumbai for his job for which Sudha had to quit her job in Kolkata to find a new one in Mumbai.

After overcoming the initial excitement both Nidhi and Sudha settled down. Sudha sighs merrily, "So Nidhi, I can't believe that finally the day has arrived and we are here with each other." Nidhi pours her excitement," Sudha, Sudha, Sudha! You know how eagerly I 've waited for this day since we fixed the meeting over phone a month ago." Sudha replies promptly, "You know I was totally surprised to hear that day that you have settled in Bangalore with you daughter and son-in-law. Just then I decided to meet you. We're in touch over social media but meeting you in person is something beyond definition." Sudha notices a sudden change in Nidhi's emotion, "What happen Nidhi? Anything wrong? "Nidhi controls herself, "No, it's okay. Actually I didn't ever imagine to settle here leaving my City of Joy. But you know Man proposes and God disposes. Sudden demise of Arun after three years of my retirement left me nowhere. He was fine with no such illness that could claim his life. But it happened." Sudha thoughtfully answers, "You know Nidhi, same thing happened with me. Immediately after my retirement we all shifted from Mumbai to

Bangalore to live with our son Akshay as he was posted with the most prestigious project with the most prestigious MNC here. But Bangalore couldn't gift Raju his life span and five years after he passed away due to a cerebral attack. There's a long pause and Nidhi sighs," It's all about destiny Sudha".

Just then the waiter comes and fixes the table with Sudha's hot chocolate, Nidhi's cold coffee and two chicken sandwiches with extra cheese and mayonese. Sudha gets much surprised, "You still remember my favourites! Oh!!! You're such a darling Nidhi." Nidhi pretends to be annoyed and asks, "Why? Don't you remember mine?" Both the friends burst into joyful laughter. Nidhi then asks Sudha, How's Akshay now? Got married yet? Or still a Mama's Boy?!!" Sudha joyfully replies," No Yaar! He's now an American citizen, his wife Dolly is a native American. They're happily married for two years but rarely visit India. Another good news Dolly is expecting and that's all. Nidhi gets serious, "And that's all? Are you joking? You came here to live with your son. Now you're saying.....
"

Sudha interrupts Nidhi, "It's not that what are you thinking. Akshay and I were doing well. A grand promotion in the office demanded him to settle in America. That lucrative offer was everything for Akshay." Nidhi nods her head," No Sudha, don't make me or yourself fool. Everything? Something more than Mom? Specially when Father is no more to stand by Mom. "Sudha gets silenced. As if something has snatched her power of words. Sudha knows very well that what Nidhi is saying is completely true. Still Sudha tries to defend after a momentary pause," It's his life and career. And I too wanted a high ambitious career for him. Leave it. What about our darling Jyothi? How's she doing?" Nidhi controls her anger against Akshay and softly answers," Yes, she's okay. You know she's not so good at studies. So after completing her graduation in commerce she tried for some government jobs, but with no results. One of Arun's friends Rajiv Verma was in Kolkata those days with his son Vivek for some professional purpose. One night they were being invited to our house when Rajivji proposed Jyothi's hand for Vivek. We, both husband and wife, always wanted a well-to-do family for Jyothi. Rajivji's proposal was just for us. Vivek has completed his Masters in Computer and is highly salaried. What else could we want for Jyothi?! So all were finalized and they were married off. Though Vivek's family lives in Indore, his office is in Bangalore. He is a software consultant with an MNC. So Jyothi is here with her husband.

Sudha's eyes shine with joy., "Good! Jyothi is a very understanding girl. Her communication skills are just awesome. Why doesn't she do anything of her own? Don't mind, but today financial independence is a must." Nidhi indifferently replies, "Yes she has started her online boutique which gets much response. Her products are receiving overwhelming responses throughout India. That's okay for her." Sudha in a ruling tone says, "What type of mother you are? Look Yaar! She's struggling to make her own empire and you Mother is just putting your thumbs down? You should stand beside her." Nidhi pacified Sudha, "Na re. It's not that. I've sold all my properties in Kolkata and invested fifty percent in her business. The remaining fifty percent is mine kept at the bank which,you may say, is my everything apart from my gratuity and husband's pension. You know Arun's colleagues in the bank helped me a lot to make the pension transfer here in Bangalore when I decided to settle here with my daughter. Vivek and Jyothi didn't want me to live alone in Kolkata in that big mansion. Vivek's parents also wanted this. They couldn't come here because of their all those lands and ancestral properties, and at that time Jyothi was pregnant and her father's demise made her mentally ill because she couldn't even travel to Kolkata for the last rites. So I've to sacrifice my very own sentiment for my in-laws' property. Besides Arun had no brother or sister to claim anything. And that was a very tough time for both Jyothi and me and we stood by each other with everyone's help. Vivek is a good person you know. He was always there by me even balancing his duties towards his own parents. No One has any allegations against him." Tears came rolling down Nidhi's eyes. Nidhi tries to control herself. Sudha interrupts Nidhi," Why are you crying? You should be proud of your daughter and Son-in-law. Really they have done the right thing at the right moment. Now look at me. I have no grievances against anyone, but you see my son left me. I still remember that day when he came with the good news that a great promotion was being put in his pocket. He was brimming with ecstatic joy; everything was happening as he wished. All were ready from accommodation to tickets. I was so much happy for him. He was always a careerist and he deserved what he received. But the smile on my face was not from my within. I tried to smile from the core of my heart but failed. I asked myself. I also wanted his success but when it came I couldn't react to it as an ideal mother should. Am I selfish? I controlled myself. An unknown fear drove me, a fear of being alone, living alone. But I never stopped him. Why should I? He has the right to live his life. But won't you think he should ask me to go with him. He should bother to take his mother with him rather leaving her alone with none to take care of her. If I can leave Mumbai for him, then why not Bangalore?" Sudha was in pool of tears, profusely sobbing and sighing," Neha, I left Kolkata, my hometown for my husband, I left Mumbai for my son, and everybody left me in Bangalore!".

Neha sits speechless. Sudha goes on," Now my son and daughter-in-law want me to join them. Dolly is expecting. Akshay has been promoted as the CEO. They are repetitively asking me to join them. But why Nidhi? I'm not going to join them. Akshay left me when I badly needed him. It was immediately after the first death anniversary of Raju, still I was struggling to accustom myself to the absence of my husband who had been always there by me. I was missing Raju badly. The whole day I wandered in the house and Raju's memories haunted me. My only solace was Akshay. With every Sundown I made myself busy cooking Akshay's favourite dishes and preparing the table. The dinner time, the conversation between mom and son was all I lived. But who knew then that Akshay had another plan and I was no where in his plan. He shared every details of his office but never ever told anything about his future planning. Now they need me in America as a caretaker? Why should I? "Nidhi has lost her words, softly says," This is not my Sudha. Where is that evergreen bubbly Sudha full of positive vibes? Go, live with them till their cisis is over. Once Dolly is over with her delivery and she becomes use to with her new motherhood, just come back. Come back to Bangalore to your Nidhi. I'll be waiting for you if my lifespan permits." Sudha stops her, "Don't say this. Seeing you, touching you and feeling you by me is like a boon to me. That positive vibes in me are not anymore. I am a lost person now. I have to think over it whether I would go or not. Give me time. My innerself is not permitting. Though I have changed a lot over those years but my innerself still speaks for me. I have now learnt to live with my new solitude. Nidhi you always felt sorry for Jyothi's career not being so bright. But perhaps you taught her the lessons of life. So today She's doing her duty well. She has learnt to live with her mother and performing her duties towards her in-laws. It was my fault, I taught Akshay to fly. I wanted a bright career for him, but I forgot to teach him to be grounded. He learned flying and flying and one day he flew away like a migratory bird with all my ambitions and pride.

PROPOSAL ACCEPTED...

1

---- Hey Dude, you're Here! I'm looking for you everywhere.

----Why? What's it?

- Hey, you look serious. Are you okay?

- Yeah. Now open up.

- I think you are not in the mood to listen what I'm going to tell you. You're not in the right track.

----Please go on. Or else you can leave.

- Okay, as you wish. Coming weekend we're planning a trip to Agra. It's the new moon time and the Taj Mahal will be shinning.

- So? What am I to do? Am I going to arrange the tickets?

----What's wrong with you Yaar? You're just joining us. It's been finalized and I'm here only to inform

you so that you can pack your bag.

- I am not going. This time it's not possible. Please don't force me.

- Then come and say it in the group this evening. This is the last year we'll be going together. With the finals fast approaching and a high profile job in our pocket, we're going to be busy after three months. Job-training, joining and you know those extra pressure? And you're saying.........

----Please Ankit, Don't ask me again. At least this time Yaar. I'm not in the mood.

----Listen Satish, we understand it. But one thing you know, we've a plan.

----No, not again. No more plan this time. I think I've become a bully to you guys. Everywhere I go,

there is a question if I've been successful in settling those matters or not?

- What do you think you're behaving normally? Sitting like this with a face of languish, redeemed eyes won't make any differences?

----So, you think I should cheer up and make fun and celebrate.

----Yes, you should. After a few months you'll be an IITian with a high profile job settled in Mumbai,with well furnished accommodation, a handsome salary and a four- wheeler. And if everything's alright, next year you'll be in USA. You should be happy for your parents, happy for yourself. Don't you think you're getting too self-centred?

- I know Ankit. Mom and Dad are very happy with my job. They 're very excited. But.......

- No ifs and buts. You're coming and that's final. We friends will have a gala time Satish. And I promise that together we will try to chalk out a plan to solve your problem.

2

As planned, a group of ten IITians from Kanpur, including six boys and four girls have left for Agra. They're all very happy because they've all bagged job with different prestigious institutes spread all over the world through on campus interview. It's Satish among them who has got the highest salaried job in the batch. Even the professors are very happy with Satish who as an obedient student and soft-spoken boy, has always won everybody's heart.

But our Satish is very upset. For the last two years he is seeing a girl just junior to him, secretly. The word "secretly" has lost its true flavour. The secret passion for the junior girl Yasmita is known to Satish's close friends in the final year computer engineering batch. Now before parting they 're all trying whole heartedly to settle the matter.

Yasmita, belonging to the same department, us a very sweet girl and at the same time intelligent enough to be attracted. A Frank, bubbly and extrovert girl Yasmita has a golden heart full of virtue and generosity. Satish has been in love with these qualities of Yasmita bit has never showed any courage to express his feelings towards her. He has always feared about the reputation or being rejected.

Now with three months to go, Satish's friends are trying to open up everything to Yasmita. Still Satish is afraid of being denial. He himself has tried to speak to Yasmita but without success. Ankit, Satish's best friend, has a plan. He has arranged this two-day trip to Agra to chalk out the plan. After a day long side-seeing journey, they are now gossiping in the garden of the lodge.

Ankit---- Now this is the time Satish should speak out to Yasmia.

Tanvi---- Are you sure, Yasmita will accept our Satish? Actually Satish is so introvert and Yasmita, being the opposite........

Tamanna---- Aree yaar, don't you know opposite attracts.

Ankit---- Listen friends, seriously. I've a plan.

Ranjit---- Now speak. You're taking time. Can't you see Satish's condition is getting worsen.

Ankit---- We're going to take advantage of our farewell concert. Satish is our main singer. With the guitar in his hand, he is just awesome. On the stage he'll so g his own predicament.

Tamanna---- Daffar!! And you think Yasmita will understand readily that Satish has some feelings for her.!!

Everybody present there start laughing and express their disapproval. But Ankit has his own logic,

"Yasmita loves the guitar. I have seen her playing during leisure. Even her bestie Supriti has confirmed it that Yasmita likes Satish's singing style."

Ranjit---- So you had this information and what have you done with this info?

Ankit---- I had to plan and now that I have a plan, I've shared it with you all.

Shekhar---- Stupid! Do you think singing a love song on a guitar is appropriate to propose a girl like Yasmita?

Ankit---- So what else can be done?

Ranjit---- No, there is a point in Ankit's plan. If we can make Yasmita understand that Satish's song is dedicated to her, it can help.

Tanvi---- Great, by this time I'll try to know what Yasmita really feels about Satish.

Ankit----- Since it is a departmental farewell arranged only by the computer-engineering students,

it'll be easier for us. If it were to sing in front of the whole college, it would be tough enough. So I think it's a great chance for Satish. Satish dear, what do you say about it?

Satish (slowing nodding his head) ---- I've no idea. Yasmita is a different type.

Tamanna---- I have an idea Satish. You directly call her parents. Your high profile job, your Mumbai base and shifting to abroad next year---- everything is in your favour. And what else a parent can ask for a son-in-law like you!!!! (laughs softly)

Ranjit---- Don't make fun of our Satish.

Tamanna----Hey! It's not so serious you're making it. Satish is also my friend.

Ankit----- Okay okay, Don't you two start again. Let Satish speak what he wants. Satish, please dear! What do you think speak up?

Satish----- I like your idea Ankit. Surely I'll sing but this time not my composition. I'll sing some classic. Perhaps it may be the last chance.

Tanvi----- Satish! we'll manage the rest Yaar! You just go on and concentrate on what you'll sing.

That hotel manager turns up all of a sudden and asked them to leave, "You guys are too late. Please go inside. You should follow our rules and regulations." The students drop the matter for that day.

3

The day has arrived at last. Everybody is in a festive mood. The final year students of computer engineering have gathered in the community hall. The immediate junior batch is the host of the programme. They are busy with the arrangements. Professors are also happy wit the placements and the bright future of their students, specially for Satish, who has been placed sir th Google. In his inauguration speech HOD Sir also congrats Satish and wish him a bright professional career. The whole department is celebrating their success. Professors are hopeful for the next batch also. Ankit, from the parting batch, performed a heart-touching recitation from his own composition on his college, respected Sirs and his loving friends and junior mates. The whole audience cheers him with great applause. After some solo and group performances there is the announcement—"Dear students, please put your hands together for our Satish who is going to pour his heart through some melody of his choice." The hall becomes dark and the spotlight gradually follows the footsteps of Satish until he comes in the centre of the stage with his fingers on the string of his guitar. The fingers start moving with the strings weaving a spontaneous melody through Satish's voice with the help of Stevie Wonder's

"No New Year's day to celebrate
No chocolate-covered candy hearts to give away

No first of spring No song to sing

In fact, it's just another ordinary day

No April rain

No flowers bloom

No wedding Saturday within the month of June

But what it is, is something true

Made up of these three words that I must say to you

I just called to say I love you

I just called to say how much I care

I just called to say I love you

And I mean it from the bottom of my heart

No summer's high

No warm July

No harvest moon to light one tender August night

No autumn breeze

No falling leaves

Not even time for birds to fly to southern skies

No Libra sun

No Halloween

No giving thanks to all the Christmas joy you bring

But what it is, though old, so new

To fill your heart like no three words could ever do

I just called to say I love you........

Satish just stops and the audience burst out into unbound gratification. Echoing of clapping brings tears to Satish's eyes, but he controls himself and gets down from the stage to his seat. Satish's eyes are full of tears as he takes his seat with the expected consequences to follow. Surely the song he has just sang has a universal appeal but the person for whom it has been dedicated has least idea that the song is behind sung for her. Satish is now trying to make up his mind to part from Yasmita. All his friends are sitting by his side in utter dismay. Everyone is now getting ready to leave. The anchress announces, "So, seniors, we wish you all the best and our programme has reached its ultimatum." Suddenly she stopped; with utter surprise there stands Yasmita on the stage with the microphone in her hand. She goes on saying, "Dear Seniors, please give me five more minutes and wait till the end" Satish and his group are just about to leave when they feel completely startled by Yasmita's voice. They again take their seats. A whispering goes by and by what could be the reason Yasmita makes them stop!!

4

There is now pin-drop silence in the hall. Amidst the darkness of the he'll, the spot- light is on Yasmita. It could easily be noticed that the bubbliness and the don't care charm that very much characterizes Yasmita is gone. Her face speaks of her heart's restlessness mixed with some unknown fear which is totally against her nature. Tanvi whispers, "Is it that Yasmita, so calm and quiet!" Satish looks up, takes a glance and sobs.

Yasmita starts, "Today right at this moment, I'm going to recite my own composition which is an open acceptance of my feelings, my admiration and my respect for that person who has stood beside me throughout these college years."

Satish's eyes reddens. He looks up at Yasmita. Yasmita goes on, "It was the first day, I still remembered, I was wandering at the main gate with least idea where could be the CE Department. Just then he came and led me up to here without even asking my name

- or even trying to introduce himself which could be very normal. I was surprised. Even he didn't try to flirt a little. I gradually came to know that he belongs to the same department as me.

Everyone in the Satish's group is eyeing each other, who could it be? Satish sits still with his head down. Yasmita is very much calm and quiet today as if a torpedo is on its way. Still She continues, "After that we met at the freshers' welcome. He was on the stage. His voice, his addressing sense, his attitude towards junior was awesome. Everyone knows that I am an outspoken, extrovert girl, but it seems that I could feel a strange quietness within me when I, by chance, come across him. During our college tours or excursions we met several times, and each time we met, the quietness within me only increased. Even before I could realize what is going on, it happened that the extrovert "I" had already surrendered to the introvert HE. Yes, I am deeply in love with him. Now that it is time to part, I have poured my heart in my open acceptance. I know he is here, and is listening me. Please accept me. I shall be waiting for your reply.

"In spite of madly being in love,

Modest I'm O my Dear, believe me!

Outspoken though, still seeking

Unifying process between me-n-you

Immaculate from my utter presence Tangible for you always, but Anchor To everybody except thee. Logical is My journey to thou, Occult in my all Feelings and thoughts; Voracious in My devotion towards you. So

Experience it, O Dear! From the heart.

Supreme you are O My Love!

Unique of all on the Earth.

Prime importance of my heart,

Royal guest in my little heart.

Intimate in my extreme solitude,

Young in all your lovely attitudes.

Oracle! Is this wrrong to love you?"

There is a long pause. Yasmita concludes, "That's all. Bye everyone."

Yasmita goes down the stage. Each and everyone stands up, but there is no applause. The flavour of the farewell ceremony has taken an unexpected turn. The hall is now getting empty. Satish's friends do not know what to say to Satish., only they could leave him on his own for a while. Ankit softly touches Satish, "sit a while! we're waiting for you outside." Tanvi pats Satish on his back and one by one they walk out. Satish is now sitting like a statue. He still couldn't believe his ears, what he has just heard from Yasmita is beyond his imagination.

Another soft touch on his palm startles Satish. He looks up only to find Yasmita beside him. They both look at each other. Their silence speak everything for them. Their transparent tears assist their silence in every possible way. This fabulous speechless conversation through the tears now unites the two hearts with limitless love and adoration.

Just then the friends come in and clap happiness with joyous congratulations to the new couple. Ankit hugs Satish tightly that is undefined.

9 789354 389313